# KITTEN KISSES

# LUCY DANIELS
# Kitten
# Kisses

Illustrated by Paul Howard

Hodder
Children's
Books

a division of Hodder Headline Limited

**Special thanks to Narinder Dhami**

Text copyright © 2002 Working Partners Limited
Created by Working Partners Limited, London W6 OQT
Illustrations copyright © 2002 Paul Howard
Cover illustration by Chris Chapman

First published in Great Britain in 2002
by Hodder Children's Books

For more information about Animal Ark,
please contact www.animalark.co.uk

10 9 8 7 6 5 4 3 2 1

A Catalogue record for this book is available
from the British Library

ISBN 0 340 85121 X

Typeset by Avon Dataset Ltd, Bidford-on-Avon, Warks

Printed and bound in Great Britain by
Bookmarque

Hodder Children's Books
a division of Hodder Headline Limited
338 Euston Road
London NW1 3BH

# Contents

# 1

## *A very friendly kitten*

"I *love* Christmas!" Mandy Hope said happily. She pulled a long, shimmering strand of silver tinsel from the box of decorations. "Look, James, there's loads of this. It's going to look great on the tree."

James Hunter, Mandy's best friend, nodded. He pushed his glasses more firmly up his nose and bent over the box of

1

decorations. "I'm glad I left Blackie at home," he remarked. "He'd have tried to run off with everything!" Blackie was James's naughty Labrador puppy.

Mandy started to hang the tinsel on the tree, while James burrowed deeper into the box. "What's this, Mandy?" he asked, holding up a large plastic container.

Mandy looked down at him and grinned. "Open it and see," she told him.

James prised the lid off the container and peered inside. Then he burst out laughing. "Wooden animals to hang on the tree!" he exclaimed, tipping them carefully out on to the floor. There were dogs, cats, rabbits and even reindeer, all beautifully painted and sparkling with glitter. "They're brilliant, Mandy."

Mandy glanced round the surgery waiting-room. "Well, this *is* Animal Ark!" she pointed out. She thought that Animal Ark was the best place to live in the whole world. Her mum and dad were both vets, and the surgery where they worked was built on to the back of their cottage in the village of

Welford. Mandy was mad about animals, and she couldn't imagine living anywhere else. With Christmas not far off, her parents had said that she and James could decorate the Christmas tree in the waiting-room. As Saturday morning surgery was nearly over, they'd already made a start.

"Has my last appointment arrived yet?" asked Adam Hope, popping his head round the door of his consulting-room.

"Not yet, Dad." Mandy hung the last wooden animal on the tree and stood back to admire it. "What do you think?"

"Very nice indeed," said Mr Hope. "And the wooden animals look great, just right for Animal Ark." He smiled at Mandy and James. "Let me know if anyone turns up with a reindeer, will you?"

Mandy and James laughed as Mr Hope disappeared back into his room.

"Look, James! It's snowing again." Mandy pointed excitedly at the window. The village was already covered with a thick blanket of snow, and now even more large, white flakes were falling silently from the grey sky.

"I can't wait for Christmas," James sighed, as Mandy searched through the box of decorations again. "There's *still* a week to go. That's ages."

"But there's lots of exciting things happening before Christmas," Mandy reminded him, pulling out a large silver star. "Don't forget, there's the Christmas party at school next Thursday."

"Oh, yes," James said happily. "*And* we've got that special surprise at the party. Everyone at school's talking about it."

"What do you think it can be?" Mandy asked. She fetched a chair, and stood on it to fix the star carefully to the top of the tree.

James shrugged. "I don't know," he replied. "But—"

"I know," Mandy broke in teasingly. "You can't *wait*!"

Suddenly the front door opened and a flurry of snow swept into the warm waiting-room. A dark-haired girl in a red coat hurried in, followed by a tall man carrying a cat basket. Snow dusted their outdoor clothes like icing sugar, showing that they had walked through the village to the surgery.

James nudged Mandy as the girl and her father went over to the receptionist's desk, unwinding their scarves and pulling off their gloves. "That's Tina Cunningham and her dad," he whispered.

Mandy nodded. Tina was in James's class at school, and she had riding lessons at the local stables where Mandy went

5

to Pony Club. But she was quite shy, so neither Mandy nor James knew her very well.

"We'd better fetch Jean," Mandy said to James. Jean Knox, the Animal Ark receptionist, had popped into the store cupboard to do some stock checking before the Christmas holiday.

"I'll go," James offered, and he hurried across the waiting-room.

Mandy hurried over to the Cunninghams and smiled at Tina, who returned the smile shyly. "Hello there," she said. "Jean won't be long."

"Sorry we're late," Mr Cunningham apologised. "Peaches hid behind the sofa and we couldn't get her out!"

"Peaches? What a lovely name," Mandy said, peering eagerly into the cat basket. An adorable kitten stared back at her with big, unblinking green eyes. Her thick coat was a beautiful ginger colour marked with darker marmalade stripes.

"Oh, isn't she gorgeous?" Mandy gasped, turning to Tina.

Tina nodded proudly, as Peaches sat up tall and began to wash herself with busy licks. "She's two months old today," she explained. "When she was born, she was the smallest of the litter, and she wasn't very well. She's a lot better now, but we've brought her for a check-up."

Mandy smiled. Tina seemed much less shy when she was talking about Peaches. She obviously loved the little kitten to bits. "Would she mind if I stroked her?" Mandy asked.

Tina and her dad looked at each other and laughed. Mandy wondered why. "Of course you can," said Tina.

Mandy pushed her fingers carefully through the wire front of the basket. Peaches immediately started to purr loudly. She rubbed her fluffy head against Mandy's hand and began licking her fingers. Mandy smiled at the feel of the kitten's rough little tongue on her skin. "I *did* have a bath this morning, Peaches," she laughed. "I don't need a wash, thank you!"

"Oh, Peaches licks *everything*," grinned

Tina, just as Jean Knox and James came back
from the store cupboard.

"Good morning," said Jean, picking up
her glasses from the desk. "It's the
Cunninghams, isn't it?"

"With Peaches," Mandy added. "James,
isn't she cute?"

James nodded and pushed his fingers into
the basket, just as Mandy had done. Purring
like an engine, the kitten pounced on James's
fingers and grabbed one of them between
her soft little pads. Then she licked it busily.

Mandy and Tina laughed at the surprised look on James's face. "Peaches likes licking things," Mandy explained.

"We think it's because her mum licked her so much when she was born," Mr Cunningham explained. "Peaches was so weak that her mum gave her lots of extra attention, and that included lots of grooming."

"Dad said it was just like a mummy kissing their baby!" said Tina. "I think that's why Peaches got better, because her mum licked her so much."

The door of the consulting-room opened, and Mandy's dad came out. "Hello again," he said to the Cunninghams, taking the notes Jean handed him. "Would you like to come through, and we'll see how Peaches is getting on?"

"There's nothing really wrong with her, is there, Dad?" Mandy asked anxiously.

Mr Hope shook his head. "No, but we've had to keep an eye on her because she was the runt of the litter. She was quite underweight at first, but she seems to be eating well now, and getting bigger."

Tina glanced at Mandy and James. "Would you like to . . ." she began hesitantly. Turning pink, she stopped and whispered something to her dad. Mr Cunningham nodded and smiled.

"Would you like to come in with us?" Tina finished in a rush, looking at Mandy and James.

"If Mr Hope doesn't mind, of course," added Mr Cunningham.

Mandy's face lit up. "Can we, Dad?" she asked.

Mr Hope nodded. "Of course," he said, pushing open the door of his consulting-room. "The more, the merrier!"

Mandy beamed as she followed Tina and Mr Cunningham inside. She'd fallen in love with the kitten already, and she couldn't wait to hear how Peaches was getting on. Although, looking at the kitten's friendly little face, there didn't seem to be *too* much wrong with her!

# 2

# *A Christmas mystery*

"Right, let's have a look at you, Peaches."
Mr Hope lifted the cat basket on to the
examining-table and began to unlatch it.
Peaches jumped to her paws and waited,
trying to lick Mr Hope's fingers as he undid
the catches.

Mandy watched as her dad swung open
the door of the basket. Peaches padded

out eagerly and looked round the room, her almond-shaped green eyes wide with interest. Then she bent her head, sniffed the table and gave it a couple of licks. Mandy and James burst out laughing.

"Peaches did that last time we came here," said Tina.

Mr Hope scooped up the kitten and held her in his hands for a moment. "She's definitely putting on weight," he said. "I can tell that she's heavier even without putting her on the scales. That's a very good sign."

"My friend's got a kitten the same age as Peaches," said Tina. "And her kitten's a bit bigger."

"Yes, Peaches still has some catching up to do," Mr Hope agreed. "But she's doing very well, Tina, so don't worry."

Mandy's dad weighed the kitten, and then carefully examined her eyes and ears. Peaches kept grabbing Mr Hope's fingers with her front paws and trying to wash them.

"Do you *ever* stop licking things, Peaches?" Mandy laughed.

"No, she doesn't!" said Mr Cunningham. "And we're a bit worried about it." He glanced at Mr Hope. "She licks everything around the house," he went on, "and she spends hours grooming herself too."

Mr Hope put Peaches down on the table, and the kitten immediately began to wash herself thoroughly, as if she'd heard every word that they'd said.

"Does it matter if she licks herself so much?" asked Tina. "It won't make her tongue sore, will it?"

"Oh, no," said Mr Hope. "But when cats swallow lots of hairs, a furball forms in their tummy. It makes them very sick."

"Oh dear." Tina looked worried.

"But Peaches' coat is quite short," Mr Hope went on. "And if you brush her regularly, it shouldn't be too much of a problem, however much she washes herself."

"I brush her nearly every day, don't I, Dad?" said Tina proudly.

"I bet Peaches tries to lick the brush, though, doesn't she?" Mandy joked, and Tina laughed.

"Yes, she does," she agreed.

Mr Hope put the kitten gently back into the basket. "Peaches might grow out of the habit of licking everything when she gets a bit older," he said with a smile. "But it won't hurt her too much. As long as you keep her away from things which aren't any good for her!"

"Did you hear that, Tina?" said Mr Cunningham, as he lifted the cat basket off the table. "You'd better be careful this afternoon when you and your mum make those Christmas decorations. I don't think glue and glitter will be very good for Peaches' tummy!"

Mandy and James both looked interested.

"What are the decorations for?" asked James. "Are they for your Christmas tree?"

Tina shook her head. "No, they're for the Christmas party at school," she explained. "My mum's helping to decorate the hall, because she's in the PTA."

Mandy remembered that the mums and dads who belonged to the Parent Teacher Association helped with the party every year.

15

"What are you going to make?" she asked.

"Oh, some paper chains and glittery stars and lots of other stuff," Tina replied. She smiled a little timidly at Mandy and James. "If you aren't doing anything else, maybe you'd like to come and help?"

"That's a good idea," said Tina's father. "The more people who are around to stop Peaches licking the Christmas decorations, the better!"

Mandy and James looked at each other in delight. "We'd love to come and help," Mandy said eagerly. "Is that all right, Dad?"

"Fine with me," replied Mr Hope, as he wiped down the table with disinfectant. "I'll let your mum know where you are." Mrs Hope had gone Christmas shopping in Walton, the nearest town to Welford. "One of us will pop round and pick you up later on."

Mandy turned to James. "Come on, let's get our coats," she said.

Mandy and James hurried into the Hopes' cottage through the connecting door and grabbed their coats, scarves and gloves. With all this snow, they needed to wrap up warmly. Then they pulled on their wellies and dashed back into the surgery, where Tina and her dad were waiting with Peaches.

"Brr!" Mandy shivered as Mr Cunningham opened the door. "It's even colder than yesterday."

The snow had almost stopped falling, and now there were only a few stray flakes drifting down here and there. It was so cold that Mandy could see her breath like a cloud in the icy air. But even though it was freezing cold, the village looked very beautiful and Christmassy with the snow glistening on the trees and the rooftops. The fields around the village were covered with a heavy layer of snow too, as if someone had hidden them under a thick, white quilt. Mandy hoped that the snow would last until Christmas Day. It didn't really *feel* like Christmas unless there was snow.

"Are you going to buy Peaches a Christmas present?" Mandy asked Tina as they walked though Welford, the fresh snow crunching under their feet.

Tina nodded. "I've been saving my pocket-money," she said. "Mum's going to take me to the pet shop in Walton to buy it."

"What are you going to get her?" James asked curiously.

"Something she can lick!" Tina smiled.

"Good idea," said Mandy, peeping into the cat basket. Tina had wrapped Peaches up snugly in her cosy blanket, and the kitten

seemed quite happy to stay there, with just her little ginger head poking out.

"Is your mum coming to the party on Thursday?" Mandy asked Tina, as they crossed the village green.

"Yes, she is," replied Tina. "She's going to put up the decorations just before, and then stay to watch the— the party," she finished.

"Oh!" James said suddenly, as if an idea had just struck him. "Tina, have you heard about the special surprise that everyone's talking about? You know, the one that's going to happen at the party?"

Mandy glanced at Tina, and was puzzled to see she had turned bright red.

"Yes, I've heard about it," mumbled Tina, her head down.

"Well, I was wondering if your mum knew what the surprise was." James stared eagerly at Tina. "I mean, she's in the PTA so maybe she knows what's going on. The teachers won't tell us *anything*."

Tina looked even more embarrassed and didn't say anything.

"I think it's better to wait until the party, don't you, James?" Mr Cunningham said quickly. "After all, it's meant to be a surprise. And it won't be if you find out beforehand!"

"Oh, OK," sighed James. "I suppose you're right."

Mandy stole a sideways glance at Tina and her dad as they walked on through the snow. James hadn't noticed anything, but it seemed to Mandy that maybe Tina and her dad had a very good idea what the big surprise was going to be! Mandy smiled to herself. It was quite a Christmas mystery . . .

# 3

## *Lost in the snow*

The Cunninghams' house was in Willow Lane, not far from Lilac Cottage where Mandy's gran and grandad lived. By the time they reached the house, Mandy's nose felt like an icicle. Even her hands in their fleecy blue gloves were numb. Mandy peeked into the cat basket again, but Peaches was still wrapped up in her blanket, and looked as warm as toast.

"Let's all go inside and have a nice hot drink," said Mr Cunningham, fumbling in his pocket for his keys. But suddenly the door opened and a tall, fair-haired woman stood on the doorstep.

"Come in," she said. "You must be freezing."

"Mum, this is Mandy and James," Tina told her, as everyone trooped into the hall. "They've come to help make the Christmas decorations."

"Oh, good," said Mrs Cunningham cheerfully. "That's very kind of you both."

Mandy unwound her scarf from round her neck. The house was warm and welcoming after the frosty air outside. She could see a log fire burning in the living-room, and a large Christmas tree stood next to the sofa, its fairy lights twinkling in lots of different colours.

"How's Peaches?" asked Tina's mum.

"She's fine," said Tina. "She's put on some more weight."

"I'll take her into the kitchen and give her

something to eat," said Mrs Cunningham, unlatching the basket and lifting out Peaches. "You go and get warm by the fire, and I'll bring you some hot chocolate."

"Oh, yum!" said James. Then he blushed when everyone smiled.

"And I've got some banana cake too," Tina's mum added, as she carried the kitten off towards the kitchen. "Now, Peaches, don't lick my hair. I've told you about that before!"

"Come on in," said Tina, leading Mandy and James into the living-room as Mr Cunningham disappeared upstairs. There was a large table at one end of the room, covered with sheets of coloured foil and card, tubes of glitter, paints, scissors and glue.

"It looks like Mum's got everything ready," said Tina excitedly.

"What shall we make first?" Mandy asked, sitting down on one of the chairs.

"Well, paper chains are quite easy," replied Tina.

"I can do that," offered James. "We made them at school last year."

"Shall we make some stars, Tina?" Mandy suggested. "If we cut them out of card, then we could cover them with glitter."

"Good idea," Tina agreed.

James collected some sheets of foil and started cutting them into strips. Meanwhile, Mandy and Tina each took a pencil and tried to draw some stars on a piece of card. But it was much more difficult than it looked.

"This is awful!" Mandy sighed, staring at the third wobbly star she'd just drawn. "I can't get it right, even with a ruler."

"It's really hard to get the star the same size all round," complained Tina. "Look, mine's got three tiny points and three big ones!"

Just then Tina's mum came in with a tray, bearing three steaming mugs of hot chocolate, as well as a large rectangular cake sliced into chunks. "Oh, you've started already," she said with a smile, putting the tray down on the table. "Goodness me, James, that looks marvellous."

James grinned and held up his paper chain. He was using three colours, red, green and

silver, and he'd already made quite a long chain by looping the foil strips and gluing them together.

"We're not doing very well, Mum," said Tina gloomily, pointing at the piece of card she was drawing on.

"Our stars don't look a bit like stars," Mandy added.

"Well, maybe I can help," said Tina's mum, picking up a pencil. Mandy and Tina drank their hot chocolate and watched closely as Mrs Cunningham drew a large triangle on a thick piece of card and cut it out.

"But that doesn't look anything like a star!" protested Tina. Mandy was secretly thinking the same thing.

"This is just a template to draw round," Mrs Cunningham replied. "Now comes the magic part." She put the triangle on top of another piece of card and drew round it. "That makes three points of the star," she explained. Then she turned the triangle upside-down, and placed it on top of the first one so that it made the other three points of the star. "And there you are," Tina's mum went on, lifting the template off the card. "Not a bad-looking star, even if I say so myself!"

"That's great, Mrs Cunningham," Mandy said admiringly. "We can make loads of stars now!"

Mrs Cunningham made another triangle template, and Mandy and Tina set to work again. Mandy was just proudly completing her very first star when she felt something licking the leg of her jeans. She jumped, and dropped the tube of glitter she was holding.

"Oh!" she gasped, bending down to look under the table. Peaches was sitting there, looking very pleased with herself. She stared up at Mandy with a loud *miaow*.

"Peaches, what are you doing here?" scolded Tina, leaning down to scoop up the kitten. "I thought you were in the kitchen."

"Don't let Peaches anywhere near the decorations," warned Mrs Cunningham, as the kitten tried to wriggle her way out of Tina's arms. The shiny foil that James was using had caught Peaches' attention, and she was staring at it as it shimmered in the light.

"I'd better take her back to the kitchen." Tina stood up, but suddenly Peaches struggled free and leaped out of Tina's arms on to the table. She landed right on top of the glittery star that Mandy had just made, getting a few bits of loose glitter on her paws.

"Don't let her lick it!" Mandy cried in alarm. She made a grab for Peaches, and managed to get hold of her before she had a chance to lick anything. But by this time she had bright silver glitter on her ears too, and on the tip of her tail.

"She looks like a fairy kitten!" Mandy laughed.

"I'll take her into the kitchen and get her cleaned up," said Mrs Cunningham, taking charge of Peaches. "Call me if you need any help."

For the next hour, Mandy, James and Tina worked very hard on the decorations. James made three long paper chains, and Mandy and Tina drew a whole row of glittering stars. They also made some jolly Father Christmasses, painting them red and using fluffy white cotton wool for Santa's beard.

"I think that's quite enough for today," said Mrs Cunningham, coming back into the living-room and surveying the busy table. "Well done, all of you. Bring the decorations into the kitchen, and we'll dry them off. I've made some sandwiches for lunch."

Mandy, James and Tina carefully collected up everything they'd made and carried them into the kitchen. Peaches was curled up cosily in her basket by the Aga, but she lifted her head and mewed with delight when she saw them. Mrs Cunningham began to lay the decorations on top of the stove. The stove lids were down, covering the hotplates, so that the decorations wouldn't get too hot. Meanwhile Mandy, James and Tina sat at the kitchen table to have their lunch.

"What shall we do now?" asked Tina, when they'd finished all the sandwiches.

"We could go outside and build a snowman," James suggested.

"Good idea!" said Mandy and Tina together.

Mandy looked out of the back door as she pulled on her wellies. The snow had stopped falling, but it looked quite deep. They'd be able to make a brilliant snowman.

"Will Peaches come outside with us?" she asked.

Tina shook her head. "No, she hates the snow," she replied, unlocking the back door. "She'll probably watch us through the door."

They went outside and closed the door behind them. Mandy laughed when, a

moment later, she saw Peaches bound out of her basket and rush over to peer through the glass panel at the bottom of the door.

"Look, she's licking the glass!" Mandy pointed out with a grin.

James was already rolling a snowball around the lawn, making it bigger and bigger. "Come on, you two," he called.

They set to work. It didn't take the three of them long to roll a big, round ball of snow for the snowman's body, and then a smaller one for his head.

"We need some pebbles to make his nose and eyes," Mandy said. While James and Tina lifted the snowman's head on to his body, she went off to find some pebbles. Most of the garden was covered with snow, but she spotted a gravel path at the side of the house. Because it was quite sheltered, the snow wasn't as deep here, and the gravel was showing through.

Mandy walked over to the side of the house, leaving a trail of footprints in the clean, white snow. There was a large woodpile on the other side of the path, the logs neatly stacked one on top of the other. Tina's dad must have been very busy cutting wood for their fire, Mandy thought as she bent down to pick up some stones.

"*Mee-ow*!"

Mandy smiled when she heard the kitten's voice. Peaches must have ventured outside after all. "Peaches?" she called, expecting to see the little kitten appear round the side of the house. But there was no sign of her.

"*Meeow*!"

Mandy's eyes widened as she heard the kitten calling again. Where was that noise coming from? It sounded as if it was close by.

There was another soft mew. It was coming from the woodpile! Mandy dashed over and peered round the end of it. At once her heart began to beat faster. There, curled up on a grubby piece of cardboard between the woodpile and the fence, were three tiny kittens.

# 4

# *The missing mum*

"Oh!" Mandy clapped a hand to her mouth in surprise. She stared down at the three kittens, who huddled together, shivering. Mandy could tell that they weren't very old because their eyes weren't fully open yet. One was black, one was white with ginger patches and the third was a beautiful smoky grey with darker stripes.

"Oh, you poor things," Mandy whispered, a lump in her throat. She turned round and shouted down the garden. "Tina! James! Come here, quick!"

"What's the matter?" asked James, hurrying over with Tina close behind.

"Look." Mandy pointed behind the woodpile at the kittens, and James and Tina both gasped.

"Are they all right?" Tina said anxiously.

"Where's their mum?" asked James.

"I don't know, but we need to get them inside and warm them up," Mandy said urgently.

"I'll go and tell Mum," said Tina, and she ran off round the side of the house.

"They look cold," James said in a worried voice.

"Let's wrap them in our scarves," Mandy suggested. She squeezed behind the woodpile and bent down to pick up the black kitten, who was nearest. The kitten mewed loudly as Mandy handed it to James, followed by the ginger and white one.

While James was settling the first two

kittens snugly inside his jacket, Mandy reached for the tiny, smoky grey kitten. She bit her lip as she lifted it up and felt how thin it was. Quickly she wrapped the kitten in her warm blue scarf, just as Tina ran round the side of the house towards them.

"Mum says to bring the kittens straight in," she panted. "And your mum's just come, Mandy."

Mandy felt a rush of relief. Her mum would be able to tell if the kittens needed any treatment.

Mrs Cunningham and Mrs Hope were waiting for them by the back door. "Come inside, quickly," said Mrs Cunningham, opening the door wider. "Are the poor little things all right?"

"I don't know," Mandy gasped, as she and James rushed into the warm kitchen. She looked anxiously at her mum. "Oh, Mum, the kittens are *so* cold, and they're really thin, especially this one." She unwrapped her scarf and a tiny, fluffy grey head came into view. James had already undone his coat and put his two kittens down on the kitchen table.

"It looks like I arrived just in time, doesn't it?" said Emily Hope. "Let me have a look at them. Goodness me, they *are* tiny, aren't they? They can only be about four or five days old."

Everyone stood round the table watching as Mrs Hope checked the kittens over. James's kittens seemed to perk up now that they were in a warm place, and they nosed their way blindly round the table on their stumpy, unsteady legs, mewling loudly. The tiniest kitten sat in a heap, shivering. Mandy thought it looked utterly miserable.

"Well, this one's a girl," said Mrs Hope as she examined the grey kitten. "And the other two are boys. They're in remarkably good shape, considering how cold it is outside."

Mandy's heart thumped with relief.

"But they're a bit underweight, especially this one," Mrs Hope went on. She gently stroked the grey kitten's head. "She's definitely the runt of the litter."

"Just like Peaches when she was born," said Tina.

Just then there was a loud *miaow* at their feet. Mandy looked down to see Peaches standing on her back legs with her front paws against the table leg, trying in vain to see what was going on.

"Peaches wants to make friends with the kittens," laughed Tina.

"I think the kittens have had enough excitement for one day," Mandy's mum said with a smile. "It might be best to keep Peaches away from them for the moment."

"OK," agreed Tina. "I'll shut her in the

living-room." She picked up Peaches and carried her out.

"Mrs Hope, will the mother cat come back for her kittens?" asked James.

Mandy's mum frowned. "That's a good question. It's very unusual for a mother cat to abandon her kittens, but that does seem to have happened here. The kittens certainly don't look like they've been feeding regularly."

"Maybe something's happened to their mum," Mandy suggested, picking up the black kitten who had strayed too close to the edge of the table.

"Yes, that's possible," Mrs Hope agreed. "It's quite likely that the mother might need some medical attention herself." She turned to Mrs Cunningham and to Tina, who had just come back into the room. "Have you noticed any stray cats hanging about your garden?" she asked.

Tina and her mum looked at each other, then shook their heads. "No, I'm afraid not," said Mrs Cunningham.

Mandy couldn't help feeling worried all

over again. The kittens were safe, but what about their mother? She could be lying somewhere, injured or ill. "What's going to happen to the kittens now?" she asked anxiously.

"Well, they're going to need a lot of care and attention," replied her mum. "They'll have to be fed regularly for a start, as their mother isn't here to feed them."

"We could keep them here for the time being," offered Mrs Cunningham.

Tina's face lit up. "Oh, Mum, can we?" she asked, her eyes shining.

"Yes, I think so," said her mum with a smile. "It seems a shame to take them out into that snow again, that's for sure."

"Well, it would be a good solution to the problem," agreed Mandy's mum. "At least then the kittens would be here if their mum does come back."

Mandy looked at James in delight, and he grinned back at her.

"Do we have to bottle-feed them?" asked Tina, and Mrs Hope nodded.

"I can bring you some bottles and some

milk substitute," she said. "We have plenty at the surgery."

"Just tell us exactly what to do," said Mrs Cunningham, going over to her larder. "I've got a cardboard box in here that would make a warm bed," she went on, pulling open the door. "And, Tina, there are some old towels in the bottom of the airing-cupboard. Could you fetch them, please?"

"The kittens look tired," Mandy said, as Tina dashed out of the kitchen. The grey kitten yawned, showing her pink tongue and tiny white teeth. Even the two boys had stopped roaming around and were sitting quietly, leaning against each other.

When Tina came back, Mandy and James helped her to tuck the towels into the cardboard box her mum had found. The box was big, and quite deep so that the kittens couldn't climb out. James and Tina each put one of the boys on to the soft towel, and then Mandy gently popped their little sister down next to them. All three snuggled up cosily together, and in a moment they were all fast asleep.

"We ought to give them names," Mandy said.

"I was thinking about that," said James. "What about Freckle for the one with the patches? He's got a few small spots right next to his nose!"

"I'd like to call the black one Banjo," said Tina. "My gran used to have a black cat called that."

"Mandy, why don't *you* name the other kitten?" James suggested.

Mandy stared into the box. The kitten was so pretty that she deserved a *special* name, but Mandy's mind was a complete blank. She liked the name Jasmine, but it seemed a very big name for such a tiny kitten. She thought she should choose something light and pretty and silvery-grey, just like the kitten's fur.

"I've got it," Mandy said suddenly. "How about Cobweb?"

"Perfect!" said Tina, a big smile on her face.

"That sounds lovely," said Mandy's mum. She stood up and picked up her coat. "Come

on, you two. I'll collect some bottles and milk substitute from the surgery and bring them round in a little while. Those kittens are going to be hungry when they wake up!"

"Come and see the kittens tomorrow," said Tina, as Mandy and James put on their coats.

"We will," Mandy promised.

It was the middle of the afternoon by now, and the sun was beginning to set. It was even colder than it had been in the morning, and Mandy shivered as they walked down the Cunninghams' path.

"We're going to have to walk home," said Mrs Hope. "Your dad needed the Land-rover to visit a farm."

"We don't mind," Mandy said. "We can look out for the kittens' mum while we're walking through the village," she added hopefully.

"That's a good idea," agreed James.

As they walked along the road, Mandy and James kept a sharp look-out for any cats wandering about. But there wasn't a single one to be seen. Mandy was very disappointed.

"I expect they're all indoors," said James, as they reached his house. "I know Benji will be!" Benji was James's cat.

"Yes, but if the kittens' mum is a stray, she won't have a home to go to," Mandy pointed out, biting her lip. She stared across the snow-covered green. Somewhere out there was the kittens' mum. The kittens were being looked after now, but Mandy still felt worried. Was their mother safe and well, or had something happened to her?

# 5

## *Pumpkins and puppeteers*

"Mandy, we're going over to the Cunninghams now," Mrs Hope called from the kitchen. "You and James had better get your coats and wellies on."

"OK," Mandy called back. She hurried out of the living-room with James behind her. It was the following day, and James had come over for Sunday lunch. Mrs Hope had promised that she would take them over to Tina's house in the afternoon, and they couldn't *wait* to see the kittens again.

Mandy and James dashed into the kitchen to get their wellies, which were standing by the back door.

Adam Hope, who was doing the washing-up, raised his eyebrows at them. "I didn't know you were so keen to help me with washing-up!" he teased.

"Oh, Dad," Mandy laughed. "You know Mum said we didn't have to, this time. We're going to see the kittens."

"I hope they're all doing well," said Mr Hope, as he rinsed a plate. "It's a shame we haven't found the mother yet."

"Maybe she'll turn up today," James said hopefully.

At that moment Mandy's mum came through the connecting door from the surgery. "I've found some more of that milk substitute," she said, holding it up. "I *thought* we had another couple of packets in the stock cupboard." Mandy and her mum had popped back to the Cunninghams the previous afternoon to drop off the bottles and milk. The kittens had still been asleep, so Mandy hadn't seen them feeding yet. She hoped that they were all drinking lots of milk, especially Cobweb. It would help her to get bigger and stronger.

"It's even colder today, isn't it?" said James, as they went outside to the Land-rover. The sun was shining and the sky was blue, but the air was still freezing and their breath hung in frosty clouds.

Mandy nodded. "It's a good thing we found the kittens yesterday," she said, looking solemn. She couldn't bear to think of them out in the cold, all alone without their mother.

When they arrived at the Cunninghams' house, Tina's mum answered the door. "Come in," she said. "I'm afraid we've got quite a lot going on today! I hope you don't mind."

Mandy wondered what she meant. "How are the kittens?" she asked.

"Doing very well," replied Tina's mum. "They're asleep at the moment, but they'll be awake for a feed very soon, I'm sure! Tina's in the living-room with Peaches." Mrs Cunningham smiled broadly, and Mandy wondered why she looked so amused. "Do take off your coats and go right in."

Mandy and James were hanging up their coats, when James nudged her. "Can you hear something?" he said in a low voice.

Mandy listened hard. At first she couldn't hear anything, then, very faintly, she heard the sound of piano music tinkling away behind the living-room door. Suddenly a voice shouted, "*I am your Fairy Godmother, Cinderella!*"

Mandy laughed. "Tina must be watching TV," she said to James, as Mrs Cunningham opened the door to the living-room.

Mandy stared into the room, hardly able to believe her eyes. Tina was sitting on the sofa with Peaches on her lap, but she wasn't watching TV. The room looked completely different to yesterday, when they had been making decorations in there.

The big dining-table had been moved, and

a large puppet theatre, like a Punch and Judy show but bigger, stood at one end of the living-room. The theatre was brightly painted, and it had a wide stage with red velvet curtains at each side. On the stage were two puppets, a beautiful, golden-haired fairy in a shimmering silver dress, and a girl dressed in rags. At the front of the stage was a big, round pumpkin.

As Mandy and James watched open-mouthed, the fairy announced, "You *shall* go to the ball, Cinderella!" She tapped the pumpkin with her silver wand. There was a flash of pink smoke and a loud BANG, which made Mandy and James jump. As the smoke drifted away, Mandy realised that the pumpkin had gone. A gleaming golden coach stood in its place!

"Isn't it great?" said Tina, jumping up with Peaches in her arms. She laughed when she saw the looks of amazement on Mandy and James's faces.

"Where did all *this* come from?" gasped James, staring at the puppet theatre.

There were rustling noises from behind the theatre, and suddenly two people popped out, grinning. One was a tall, fair-haired man in his early twenties, who looked a bit like Tina's mum, and the other was a young woman with silver-rimmed glasses and a shock of ginger hair.

"This is my brother Matthew," said Mrs Cunningham. "And his girlfriend, Alex."

"We're puppeteers," explained Matthew.

"In case you hadn't guessed!" his girlfriend added.

"Wow!" James's eyes were shining. "I've never met a puppeteer before."

"Me neither," said Mandy, staring at the puppet theatre with interest. "Are you doing a show in Welford?"

Matthew and Alex laughed and exchanged a glance.

"Mum, please can I tell Mandy and James the secret?" begged Tina. "I'm sure they won't tell anybody else."

"I think we'll have to," replied Mrs Cunningham, her eyes twinkling. "They'll be coming round to see the kittens, so they're bound to find out sooner or later!"

"Find out what?" Mandy and James said together.

"Uncle Matt and Alex are going to do their puppet show at the school Christmas party," Tina burst out. "*That's* the big surprise!"

"Oh!" James looked thrilled. "That'll be great, won't it, Mandy?"

"Brilliant!" Mandy agreed. "Is it the story of Cinderella?"

"That's right – hence the pumpkin!" laughed Matt. "We're staying here for the next few days, so you'll probably see a few more rehearsals. But remember, not a word to anyone! The teachers want to keep it a secret."

"We promise," Mandy grinned.

"I liked the special effects," said James. "How did you make all that smoke?"

"We've got some special smoke bombs," Matt explained. "When we set them off, it gives us just enough time to get the pumpkin off stage, and put the coach in its place."

"You were really quick," said James admiringly.

"We have to be," Alex told him. "It takes two of us to get the coach into position, so we have to take the puppets off our hands, then put them back on again really fast."

"We've got quite a few other tricks up our sleeves too," added Matt, "but you'll have to wait until the Christmas party for those!"

"I might pop over to the party myself,"

Emily Hope said with a smile. "The show looks marvellous."

"It's coming along nicely," replied Alex. "As long as we keep the puppets away from Peaches. She got hold of Cinderella this morning, and nearly licked her to bits!"

Everyone looked at Peaches who was lying in Tina's arms, busily licking one of her fingers.

"Has Peaches met Cobweb, Freckle and Banjo yet?" Mandy asked, tickling the kitten's soft, apricot-coloured tummy.

"Not yet," replied Tina. "We decided to keep them away from each other until the kittens are feeling better."

"Talking of the kittens, I'd better go and make up their bottles," said Mrs Cunningham, and she hurried off to the kitchen.

"It was you who found the kittens, wasn't it, Mandy?" asked Alex. "Tina told us all about it."

Mandy nodded. "Yes, I heard one of them mewing when we were in the garden."

"Thank goodness you did," said Alex.

"They're gorgeous, aren't they? I was playing with Banjo and Freckle this morning. They're pretty lively considering they're still so young."

"Let's go into the kitchen and see them," suggested Tina. "I'd better leave Peaches in here, though."

She put Peaches on the sofa, and they all went out of the living-room. Mandy couldn't help laughing at the kitten's face. She looked very cross at being left behind!

Mrs Cunningham was at the worktop, whisking some yellow milk powder in a jug of warm water. She turned and smiled as everyone came in. "They're just waking up," she said.

Mandy and James bent eagerly over the cardboard box. Banjo and Freckle were already awake and mewing for attention, scrambling to get out of the box. Cobweb was still half-asleep and yawning.

"Oh, their eyes have opened!" Mandy said, delighted. "Look, Banjo's and Freckle's are green."

"This one's my favourite," said James, scooping up Banjo. "He's so naughty!" He waggled his fingers, and the kitten grabbed them and clung on like a little monkey.

"I love them all," said Tina, giving Freckle a cuddle.

"Come on, Cobweb." Mandy lightly tickled the kitten's grey head. "Are you going to wake up? It's time for your feed."

Cobweb yawned again, and slowly opened her blue eyes. Now that they were fully open, they looked huge, and sparkled like sapphires.

"She's so pretty, isn't she?" said Tina. "Can we feed them now, Mum?"

Mrs Hope and Mrs Cunningham handed out the bottles and Mandy, James and Tina sat down, each with a kitten in their lap. James had Banjo, Tina had Freckle and Mandy had Cobweb. Freckle and Banjo grabbed at the bottles, and began to suck greedily straightaway. But Cobweb didn't seem very interested, and she pulled away from the rubber teat after just a few mouthfuls.

"Come on, Cobweb," Mandy urged, trying gently to push the teat back into the kitten's mouth. "Have a bit more."

But the kitten turned her head away every time Mandy moved the bottle towards her. Feeling worried, Mandy looked over at her mum.

"We can't make her drink if she doesn't want to, love," Mrs Hope said softly. "Don't get too upset. Cobweb's weaker than her brothers, but she'll probably pick up over the next couple of days."

"I hope so," Mandy whispered, stroking the tiny kitten's back. "I really hope so."

# 6

# *Lily's special secret*

"Oh, Jean, the kittens are gorgeous," Mandy exclaimed, as she leaned against the receptionist's desk. "Cobweb's eyes are so big and blue."

"And we saw Tina today at school, and she said that they're fine," James added.

It was Monday, and James had come back to Animal Ark with Mandy after school. Mrs

Hope had promised to take them over to the Cunninghams' for a quick visit after she'd finished evening surgery. At playtime, everyone had been talking about the big surprise that was coming up at the Christmas party. Mandy and James hadn't breathed a word about the puppet show, but it was hard keeping such an exciting secret!

"It's marvellous that the kittens are getting on so well," said Jean, sorting through some files. "But what about Cobweb? I thought you were worried that she wasn't feeding properly?"

Mandy felt a pang of worry. "Tina said Cobweb's sleeping a lot, and she's still not drinking much milk."

"Well, hopefully she'll get her appetite back in a day or two," Jean said. "Isn't it quiet tonight?" she added, glancing round the empty waiting-room. "We've only got one more patient booked in. Still, I'm sure your mum and dad will be frantic enough over Christmas!"

Mandy nodded. Christmas was usually a busy time at Animal Ark because some people fed their pets too much rich food, and then they were sick.

At that moment the outside door was pushed open, and a man and a woman walked in carrying a cat basket. They came straight over to Jean's desk, looking rather worried.

"We're Mr and Mrs Devlin," said the man, resting the cat basket on the desk. "We've got an appointment to see the vet with our cat, Lily."

"Ah, yes, this is the first time you've visited us, isn't it?" said Jean.

Mrs Devlin nodded. She was young and very pretty, with curly dark hair. "That's right. We've only just moved to Welford."

Mandy couldn't resist peeping into the basket to take a look at Lily. She always loved meeting new animals! But what she saw gave her quite a shock. Lily was a young black cat, but her fur wasn't sleek and glossy. It looked matted and dirty, and she was very thin. She clawed miserably at the sides of the basket, letting out a yowl every so often. Mandy glanced at James. He was staring at

Lily too, and obviously wondering what was the matter with her.

"Can I just have your address, please?" asked Jean, picking up her pen.

"17, Willow Lane," replied Mr Devlin. Mandy wondered if they'd met the Cunninghams yet, who lived at number 21.

"Thank you," said Jean. "Do take a seat."

Mr Devlin was about to pick up the cat basket again when he noticed Mandy and James staring at Lily. "She doesn't look too good, does she?" he said sadly. "She went missing for about five or six days just after we moved here. She only came back home the day before yesterday."

"Oh, poor Lily," Mandy said.

Lily was scrabbling at the door of the cage, trying to get out of the basket. Suddenly, though, she seemed worn out, and she flopped down on her blanket with her head on her paws.

"We were so worried about her when she disappeared," Mrs Devlin chimed in, sitting down on one of the chairs. Mandy and James sat down next to her. "We thought she must have tried to go back to our old house. We couldn't believe it when she turned up on the doorstep!"

"So we've brought her in to make sure she's all right," her husband added. "She's lost so much weight, and she's just not herself."

Lily raised her head and let out another mournful howl.

"She absolutely hates being in the basket," Mrs Devlin told Mandy and James. She looked at Jean Knox. "Would you mind if we let her out?"

Jean smiled. "That sounds like a good idea," she said.

Mr Devlin opened up the basket, and Lily looked a little more cheerful. She padded her way out on to Mrs Devlin's lap and stretched over to sniff at Mandy. Instead of settling down on her owner's knees, she stepped on to Mandy's lap, turned round a few times and then lay down, purring very faintly.

"Well!" Mrs Devlin laughed. "Lily's really taken to you. I'm sorry, I don't know your name."

"I'm Mandy Hope," said Mandy, gently stroking Lily's thin back. The cat had closed her eyes, and looked as if she was already half-asleep. "And this is my friend James Hunter. My mum and dad are the vets here."

"Well, no wonder you're good with animals," Mr Devlin said with a smile. "Lily doesn't take to just anybody, you know!"

The door to the consulting-room opened and Mandy's mum came out. She looked rather surprised to see Mandy sitting there with a cat on her lap. "Hello, you must be the Devlins," she said, coming towards them. "And this must be Lily."

"She doesn't like being in the basket," Mr Devlin explained. "But she seems to like sitting on Mandy's lap."

"So I see!" smiled Emily Hope. "She looks so comfortable, I hardly like to disturb her. Mandy, would you carry Lily into the surgery, please? That's if Mr and Mrs Devlin don't mind?"

"Of course not," said Mrs Devlin, standing up.

Mandy picked up Lily and carried her

across the waiting-room. The cat hardly stirred, and her eyes stayed closed. She seemed so weak and tired. Mandy hoped that there was nothing seriously wrong with her.

As the Devlins and James followed Mandy into the treatment-room, Mr Devlin explained to Mrs Hope how they had lost and found their cat.

"We don't know where she's been for the last four or five days," he said. "But she obviously hasn't been eating much, as she's got so thin."

"I feel awful now because we actually put Lily on a diet a few weeks ago," said Mrs Devlin, biting her lip. "She was really getting quite tubby."

Mandy put Lily carefully down on the examining-table. The cat crouched there, blinking her green eyes, too weary to look round the room or sniff at the table.

"Poor Lily," said Mrs Hope gently. "She does look quite miserable, doesn't she? If you say she was getting fat just a few weeks ago, I wouldn't have expected her to be quite so thin now. Four or five days without food wouldn't make that much difference. Let's see if we can find out what's wrong with her."

After a few moments, Mrs Hope raised her head and looked at the Devlins. "I can tell you exactly why Lily was getting bigger a few weeks ago," she said. "She was expecting kittens!"

The Devlins gasped, and Mandy and James looked at each other in surprise.

"And I'd say she had the kittens about a week ago," Mandy's mum added.

"But Lily's hardly more than a kitten herself!" Mr Devlin exclaimed. "She's not even a year old."

"Cats can get pregnant from around six months old," Mrs Hope told him. "So Lily is just about old enough to have had her first litter."

Mrs Devlin was frowning and looking worried. "But if Lily *has* had kittens," she said, "where on earth could they be?"

Mandy's hand flew to her mouth as an idea suddenly popped into her head. Could it be the answer? Everything seemed to fit. "Mum!" she gasped. "Do you think Cobweb, Banjo and Freckle could be Lily's missing kittens?"

# 7

## *Cobweb in trouble*

Mandy could hardly contain her excitement as she looked eagerly at her mum. Surely there was a good chance that the kittens might be Lily's? After all, the Cunninghams lived very close to the Devlins. Lily could easily have made her way into Tina's garden to have her kittens if she was lost.

"It's certainly possible," agreed Emily Hope.

"Well done, Mandy!" said James, patting her on the back.

The Devlins were looking completely confused.

"Does this mean you *know* where Lily's kittens are?" asked Mr Devlin.

Quickly Mandy explained how they'd found a litter of tiny kittens in Tina's garden, only two doors away from the Devlins' house.

"Of course, we can't be sure that they're Lily's kittens," Mandy's mum warned. "But it seems likely, I must say."

Mrs Devlin was looking very excited. "What colour are they?" she asked.

"Banjo's black, like Lily," replied James. "And Freckle is white with ginger bits."

"And Cobweb's a beautiful smoky grey tabby," Mandy added.

Mrs Devlin turned to her husband. "I know kittens don't always look like their parents," she said, "but Lily's mum was a silver tabby, which sounds just like Cobweb. Remember, David?"

Mr Devlin nodded. "They *must* be Lily's kittens," he said.

Mandy felt a thrill of excitement run through her, and she gave James a look of delight. They'd found the kittens' mum!

"I wonder why Lily abandoned her babies, though," Mr Devlin went on, sounding puzzled.

"She probably didn't mean to," replied Mrs Hope. "She might have gone looking for food for herself, and then realised that she was close to home. And I suppose once you got her back, you didn't let her out again, so she couldn't return to the kittens even if she wanted to."

"That's right," Mr Devlin agreed. "She looked so thin and ill that we couldn't bear to let her out into the snow."

"Poor Lily. She must have been desperate to get back to her babies." Mrs Devlin stroked her cat's head and glanced at Mandy. "Are the kittens doing all right without their mum?"

"Banjo and Freckle are fine," Mandy replied. "But Cobweb was the smallest and she's still a bit weak. She's not feeding very well either."

"Oh, dear." Mrs Devlin looked worried. "David, we'd better collect the kittens from the Cunninghams right away and take them home with us. Maybe Cobweb will get better when she's back with her mum again."

"I'm afraid that might not be a good idea, Mrs Devlin," Emily Hope broke in.

Mandy looked at her mum in surprise, wondering what she was going to say. Surely it was *much* better for Cobweb to be back with Lily?

"Lily hasn't been eating enough over the last few weeks, partly because she was on a diet and partly because she got lost," Mandy's mum continued. "That means she isn't making any milk, so she won't be able to feed the kittens herself."

Mandy felt bitterly disappointed.

"Oh, dear." Mr Devlin looked disappointed too. "Well, can't Ruth and I feed the kittens, like the Cunninghams are doing?"

"Yes, of course," Mandy's mum agreed. "But they need frequent regular feeds, so one of you will have to be at home all the time."

The Devlins looked at each other. "Hmm, that wouldn't be easy," said David Devlin with a frown. "You see, we both work all day."

"Well, maybe the Cunninghams wouldn't mind keeping the kittens, just for the next few weeks," Mandy's mum suggested. "I could ask them, if you like."

Mandy's face lit up as the Devlins nodded gratefully.

"It would be very kind of them," said Mr Devlin. "And we could always pop round and give them a hand in the evenings and at weekends."

"Do you think they'd mind if we visited them right now?" asked Mrs Devlin. "I'm dying to see Lily's babies!"

"We're going over there now ourselves," said Mrs Hope. "Would you like to come with us? I could introduce you to the Cunninghams, and then we can decide together what to do about the kittens."

Mr Devlin frowned. "What are we going to do if the Cunninghams *can't* keep them?" he asked.

"Let's wait and see," said Mrs Hope sensibly. "Meanwhile, I'd like to keep Lily here for a couple of days so I can put her on a drip. That will help to build up her strength again. And perhaps you should think about making sure Lily doesn't have any more kittens. The operation is very straightforward."

"Just tell us when Lily's well enough, and she can have the operation at once," said Mrs Devlin.

"You could also consider having her microchipped," Mrs Hope added. "Then you're much more likely to get her back if she goes missing again."

James turned to Mandy as Mrs Hope picked up Lily to take her into the residential unit. "Isn't this *brilliant*?" he said happily. "I can't wait to tell Tina. She's going to be so pleased that we've found the kittens' mum."

Mandy nodded. "I know," she agreed. "I just wish Lily was well enough to feed Cobweb, though. Then she might have started getting better and putting on weight."

James's face fell. "I hadn't thought of that. Maybe she'll be OK anyway."

"I hope so," Mandy replied.

Mrs Hope carried Lily through to the large room at the back of the surgery where overnight patients were housed. Mandy, James and the Devlins watched as Mrs Hope settled Lily in a large, comfortable cage and attached a drip to her front leg. Lily seemed sleepy again, and her green eyes were already closing as everyone tiptoed out of the room.

"She's going to be fine," said Mrs Hope. "Now, shall we go over to the Cunninghams'?"

Everyone put on their coats, and they set off through the village. It was a dark and frosty night, and stars twinkled overhead. There were brightly-lit Christmas trees in the living-room window of almost every house, and some people had strung fairy lights on the trees in their front gardens. Mandy had almost forgotten about Christmas in the excitement over the kittens, but now she thought that the best present of all would be if Cobweb started getting better.

"We'll have to think about finding new homes for the kittens when they're old enough," said Mrs Devlin, turning to her husband as they crossed the village green.

"James and I could help," Mandy offered. "We could put up posters in Animal Ark, and at school."

"Thank you. What a good idea," smiled Mrs Devlin.

They arrived at the Cunninghams' house and Mrs Hope rang the bell. Tina answered

the door with Peaches tucked under her arm. She looked surprised to see so many people on the doorstep.

"Tina, we've got some good news," Mandy announced. "We've found the kittens' mum!"

"Oh!" Tina's face broke into a huge smile, and she hugged Peaches close to her. The kitten began to purr loudly as if she was pleased too. "That's great. Where is she?"

Before anyone could answer, Tina's mum came out of the kitchen and hurried down the hall towards them. "Did I hear someone say that you'd found the kittens' mother?" she asked.

Mr Devlin stepped forward. "Hello, Mrs Cunningham," he said. "I'm David Devlin, and my wife and I have just moved into number 17. It looks like it was our cat, Lily, who had the kittens."

"Thank you so much for looking after them," his wife added.

"Not at all!" Mrs Cunningham exclaimed. "They're adorable. Come in out of the cold, and tell us all about it."

Everyone trooped into the hall and began pulling off their outdoor clothes. As Mr and Mrs Devlin explained about Lily and how they'd lost her, Tina turned to Mandy, looking a bit disappointed. "I guess the kittens will be going home then," she said quietly. "I'm really going to miss them, especially Cobweb."

Mandy glanced over at her mum, who'd heard what Tina was saying.

"Well, we have a problem because the kittens can't go home just yet," Emily Hope said. Quickly she explained to Tina and Mrs Cunningham that Lily didn't have any milk to feed the kittens, and the Devlins were out at work all day so it would be difficult for them to feed the kittens by hand.

"That's all right," Mrs Cunningham said immediately. "We'll just keep them here for the moment, shall we?"

Mandy and James both grinned at the delighted look on Tina's face.

"We'd be really grateful," said Mr Devlin. "We can always come round and help out when we're at home."

"And we can see that you're very good with cats!" Mrs Devlin added, looking down at Peaches who was lying cosily in Tina's arms. "What's this gorgeous kitten called? She's much too big to be one of Lily's!"

"This is Peaches," Tina said shyly.

Mandy smiled as Mrs Devlin tickled Peaches under the chin and the kitten immediately gave her fingers a good lick.

"Come through to the kitchen and see the kittens," said Tina's mum. "They're awake at the moment. Well, Banjo and Freckle are."

"How's Cobweb?" Mandy asked.

Tina looked worried. "She sleeps nearly all the time," she replied.

"Is she drinking more milk yet?" said James.

"Not really," sighed Tina. "Uncle Matt tried to feed her this morning, and she only had a few drops."

They all went into the kitchen, where Matt and Alex were lying on the floor playing with Banjo and Freckle. They held pieces of string which they were dangling over the kittens' heads, and Banjo and Freckle were trying to grab them. Tina put Peaches down on the floor, and she immediately dashed over to join in the fun.

"Matt, Alex, this is Mr and Mrs Devlin from number 17," said Tina's mum. "They think that the kittens belong to their cat, Lily."

"Oh, really?" Alex beamed. "We think they're lovely. We've been playing with them almost all day, haven't we, Matt?"

Tina's uncle nodded.

"They *are* gorgeous, aren't they?" said Mrs Devlin. "This one looks just like Lily." And she picked up Banjo and gave him a cuddle.

"Banjo and Freckle love Peaches," Tina smiled, as Freckle and Peaches began to chase each other around the table legs.

"What about Cobweb?" asked James.

"I've kept Peaches away from her so far," Tina replied. "Cobweb's so tiny, I'm scared Peaches might hurt her if she tries to play with her."

Mandy looked around for the little grey kitten. Cobweb was curled up in a tight, fluffy ball in the box, fast asleep. Mrs Cunningham had cut down the sides of the box so that the kittens could get in and out when they wanted, but Cobweb was obviously happy to stay where she was.

"Hello, Cobweb." Mandy knelt down by the box and gently touched the kitten's ears. "How are you feeling?"

Cobweb opened her big, blue eyes very slowly and lifted her head to stare at Mandy. Then she gave a little mew and curled up into a ball again.

"She doesn't want to get out of the box, or play, or do anything," Tina said sadly, keeping a tight hold on Peaches. The bigger kitten was staring curiously down at Cobweb and struggling impatiently to get out of Tina's arms.

Mr and Mrs Devlin came over to join Mandy and Tina. "Poor little thing," Mrs Devlin said quietly. She reached down and stroked Cobweb's soft grey coat, but the kitten didn't move. "I hope she'll be all right."

"So do I," Tina said in a wobbly voice.

Mandy could see that she was very upset. She'd obviously grown really fond of Cobweb. Mandy sighed, feeling very miserable. They all loved the little kitten, but there didn't seem to be anything they could do for her. How *could* they help Cobweb?

# 8

## *Peaches to the rescue*

"Only two days to go to the puppet show and the party!" chanted James. "I can't wait. It's really hard not being able to tell everyone about it. Ow!" He jumped as Banjo pounced on his foot. "Let go of my laces, Banjo!"

Mandy laughed. "He's such a pickle!" She glanced over at the box in the corner, where

Cobweb was asleep again, and sighed. "Not like Cobweb."

It was Tuesday afternoon, and Mandy and James had walked home with Tina after school to see the kittens again. Mandy had hoped that Cobweb would have cheered up a bit since the Devlins' visit the day before. But Tina told her that Cobweb was just the same, and that she'd hardly had any milk for breakfast. Mandy was getting more and more worried about the poorly little kitten. She, James and Tina had put up a poster at school asking if anyone could give the kittens new homes, but it didn't look like Cobweb would be well enough to leave the Cunninghams for a long time yet.

"Are Matt and Alex rehearsing *Cinderella* tonight?" James asked Tina.

"No, they've gone to see some friends in Walton," replied Tina. "They won't be back till late."

"Don't look so disappointed, James," laughed Mrs Cunningham. "You'll be able to see the show very soon."

"Mum and Dad are busy this evening, so

Gran's coming to collect me and James," Mandy told Tina's mum. "She'll be here about half-past five."

Tina's mum glanced at the clock. "Then we've just got time to feed the kittens before you go," she said.

"Oh, good," Mandy said. Maybe today would be the day when Cobweb finally started to feed properly. It would be lovely to see her running round and getting into mischief, just like Banjo and Freckle.

"Let's wake Cobweb up," said Tina, as her mum began to make up the bottles of milk.

Mandy, James and Tina knelt down beside the box and Mandy ruffled the kitten's grey fur with her finger. "Come on, Cobweb," she said. "Time for your dinner."

Banjo and Freckle were already sitting at Mrs Cunningham's feet, mewing loudly. They knew it was suppertime! But Cobweb didn't seem to care. She blinked her blue eyes and stayed exactly where she was.

"No, Peaches," scolded Tina as the apricot-coloured kitten padded forward

to nose curiously at Cobweb. "Leave Cobweb alone. She's much too small to play with you."

"Shall I put Peaches in the living-room?" asked James.

"Oh, thank you," said Tina, and she handed her kitten to James. "Peaches always wants to drink the milk if she stays in here at feeding-time!"

Mandy sat down at the table with Cobweb on her lap. The kitten was so tiny, she hardly weighed a thing. Tina was already feeding

Banjo, and James hurried back into the kitchen to feed Freckle, who seemed almost as hungry as his brother. But it took Mandy ages to coax Cobweb into opening her mouth so that she could pop the bottle in. Even then, the kitten only took a few sips before she stopped, mewing weakly.

"Keep trying, Mandy," Mrs Cunningham urged.

"Come on, Cobweb," Mandy said gently. "Look, your brothers have nearly finished their bottles."

"Freckle *has* finished," said James.

"So has Banjo," added Tina, holding up the empty bottle.

Mandy did her best, but Cobweb only sucked down a couple more drops of milk before she pulled away from the bottle again and stared round at everyone with big, worried eyes.

"Maybe Cobweb would feel better if there weren't so many people watching her," Tina suggested. "James, let's take Freckle and Banjo into the living-room to play with Peaches."

"OK," James agreed, and they disappeared down the hall, each with a kitten in their arms.

"I'm really worried about Cobweb," Mandy said anxiously to Mrs Cunningham. "Maybe my mum should have another look at her."

Before Mrs Cunningham could answer, Peaches bounded through the kitchen door, looking very pleased with herself. She spotted Cobweb on Mandy's lap, and, before anyone could stop her, she jumped up, right next to the tiny grey kitten.

"Peaches!" Mandy gasped, taken by surprise.

A second later, Tina and James appeared in the kitchen doorway.

"Peaches, you bad girl!" Tina scolded. "Sorry, Mandy. She was waiting by the living-room door, and she ran out when we went in with Freckle and Banjo."

"Don't let her frighten Cobweb," said Tina's mum.

But Mandy stared down at the two kittens on her lap and shook her head. "Peaches isn't frightening Cobweb," she said softly. "Look!"

Peaches was gently licking the little kitten, smoothing down the fluffy grey fur with her rasping pink tongue. Cobweb was sitting quietly, gazing up at the bigger kitten and purring more loudly than any of them had ever heard before.

"Oh!" Tina gasped. "Do you think Peaches knows that Cobweb isn't very well? Maybe that's why she's licking her, just like Peaches' mum used to lick *her*."

"And Cobweb seems to like it!" said James. "She doesn't look so miserable now."

"I'll try her with the milk again," Mandy decided. While Peaches carried on grooming Cobweb, Mandy slipped the teat into the kitten's mouth. For once, Cobweb didn't try to pull away. She started drinking the milk, and this time she kept on feeding.

"Look!" Mandy said in delight, holding up the bottle a few minutes later. "Cobweb's drunk nearly all of it."

"Thanks to Peaches," Tina added proudly, picking up her kitten and giving her a big

hug. "Cobweb loves getting kissed by her!"

"Well done, Peaches," said James.

Cobweb gave a huge yawn, showing her pink mouth and all her tiny white teeth. Mandy laid her gently back in the kittens' box. Tina put Peaches down on the floor, and the kitten immediately bounded over to the box and climbed in beside Cobweb.

Cobweb gave a pleased chirrup and the two kittens curled up together in one furry ball. As soon as they were settled, Peaches began to wash Cobweb's ears and face, licking up any stray drops of milk.

"I think Cobweb's going to be OK, don't you?" Mandy said, feeling very relieved. "She's got Peaches to look after her now."

"Thank goodness!" said James. "Tina, what about Freckle and Banjo? Shall I go and see how they're doing?"

"Oh, yes, please," said Tina. "I'd almost forgotten about them! We shouldn't have left them on their own, really."

"Don't worry, I'll go and make sure they're OK." James went off down the hall.

Mandy gazed at Cobweb and Peaches, and

smiled as she watched both kittens' eyes close peacefully. Cobweb was lucky to have a special friend like Peaches, who knew what it felt like to need lots of extra kisses.

Suddenly there was the sound of running footsteps out in the hall. A moment later James appeared in the kitchen doorway. He looked round at everyone, his eyes wide in alarm. "Come quick!" he gasped. "Banjo and Freckle have caught a mouse!"

# 9

# *Mouse alert!*

"What?" Mandy cried, jumping to her feet.

"A mouse?" repeated Mrs Cunningham. "We don't have any mice in this house."

"Are you sure, James?" asked Tina. "Banjo and Freckle aren't much bigger than a mouse themselves!"

"Come and see," replied James, turning and hurrying back to the living-room.

Mandy, Tina and Mrs Cunningham followed him quickly. James rushed over to the sofa and pointed behind it. "Look!"

The sofa was pushed against the wall, leaving a very narrow gap. Mandy bent down and peered into the space. It was very dark in there, but she could just see Freckle and Banjo playing with a small, white, furry thing with pink ears.

"It *looks* like a mouse," Tina breathed, staring over Mandy's shoulder.

"We'd better move the sofa and get rid of it," Mrs Cunningham said grimly.

But before they could do anything, Banjo grabbed the mouse in his teeth and ran out from behind the sofa. Freckle followed, mewing crossly.

"Don't let them get away!" James called anxiously. "The mouse might still be alive."

Banjo dropped the mouse proudly at Mandy's feet. Mandy crouched down to look closely at it and burst out laughing.

"What's so funny?" asked James.

Mandy picked up the mouse and held it

out. "It's all right," she said with a grin. "It's not real. It's a toy mouse!"

"Thank goodness for that," said James, grinning back.

"Oh, no!" gasped Tina, gazing at the soggy, furry mess. "It's one of Uncle Matt's puppets! They've got two mice that they turn into white horses to pull Cinderella's coach."

"Oh, dear. This one doesn't look like it could pull a coach now," said James.

They all stared down at the puppet. It had been thoroughly chewed, and the kittens' sharp little claws had torn the cloth body in several places. One of its beady black eyes and both its ears were hanging on by the merest threads.

"It's all my fault," Tina said miserably. "I shouldn't have left Freckle and Banjo in here on their own."

"Don't worry, love." Her mum put an arm round her. "I'm sure it can be fixed." She frowned at the torn puppet. "It looks quite bad, though. And Matt and Alex won't be back until late tonight, which doesn't leave them much time to mend it."

Mandy realised that Mrs Cunningham was right. The puppet would have to be mended very cleverly or the stitches would show when it was on stage. She hoped Matt and Alex could sort it out before the show.

Suddenly the doorbell rang.

"That'll probably be your gran, Mandy," said Tina's mum, glancing at the clock. She went out into the hall, and came back with Grandma Hope.

"Hello, you two." Gran smiled at Mandy and James. "Hello, Tina." Then she spotted Banjo and Freckle who were playing hide and seek under the hearthrug. "Are these the famous kittens I've been hearing about?"

Mandy nodded. "And they've been really naughty, Gran," she said, holding out the mouse. "They've chewed up one of Tina's uncle's puppets! And the show is only two days away—" Suddenly Mandy stopped. If there was one person who could sew anything back together, it was her gran!

"Oh, dear." Gran took the mouse and examined it closely. "This poor fellow's going to need quite a bit of work, isn't he?"

"Gran," Mandy began, "do you think *you* could fix him? It's really important, or Cinderella won't have *two* white horses to pull her golden coach!"

Her gran started to laugh. "Well, I don't know much about mice, but I'll have a go," she said.

Tina's face lit up. "Oh, that would be great, Mrs Hope!" she said.

"It's very kind of you, Dorothy," said Mrs Cunningham gratefully. "I know Matt and Alex will be really pleased."

"Well, the show must go on!" said Mandy's gran, her eyes twinkling. "I'll have it ready by tomorrow."

"Thanks, Gran!" said Mandy, giving her a big hug.

"Lily looks a lot better, doesn't she?" Mandy said to James. It was Wednesday afternoon. Mandy and James had just arrived at Animal Ark after school, and they had headed straight to the residential unit at the back of the surgery. Mandy's mum had said that Lily could go home today, and the Devlins had come to collect her. They were in the consulting-room, talking to Mrs Hope.

"She looks great," agreed James.

Lily was looking much healthier after two days on a drip. Her coat was glossy and her eyes were much brighter. She seemed livelier, too. She padded over to the front of the cage, purring softly, and rubbed her head against Mandy and James's fingers.

"When are we going over to Tina's?" asked James.

"After the Devlins have taken Lily," Mandy replied. "We mustn't forget to pick up the mouse from Gran on the way."

"I wonder if she's managed to fix it," said James.

"If anyone can, Gran can," Mandy promised him with a grin.

Mrs Hope came in at that moment with the Devlins close behind her. Mr Devlin was carrying Lily's basket. He and his wife beamed when they saw how much better Lily looked.

"She's almost back to her old self, isn't she?" said Mrs Devlin, stroking Lily's ear through the bars of the cage. "Thank goodness!"

"Are you ready to come home now, Lily?" Mr Devlin asked, putting the basket on the floor and opening the door.

Mrs Hope unlatched the cage, and Mandy and James laughed as Lily ran straight into her basket.

"That's the first time she's ever got into her basket without being pushed!" said Mrs Devlin. "Usually she hates it."

"She knows she's going home," said Mrs Hope with a smile. "Now, if you talk to Jean before you go, you can make an appointment for Lily to have her operation straight after Christmas. That will make sure she doesn't have any more unexpected litters of kittens! We'll microchip her then, too."

The Devlins nodded.

"Goodbye, Lily," Mandy said, watching the black cat settle down happily on her blanket. "Now just make sure you don't get lost again!"

"Gran, it's perfect!" Mandy stared hard at the mouse puppet in her hand, but she couldn't see where the eye and ears had been sewn back on. Gran's invisible mending had done the trick. "Look, James." She popped the mouse puppet on to her finger, and wiggled it at him.

"It's brilliant, Mrs Hope," said James admiringly.

"I washed it, too," said Gran, "so it's nice and fluffy again."

"This mouse is going to be the star of the show!" Mandy declared. "Thanks, Gran."

"We'd better get the puppet back to Matthew and Alex, in case they're having a last-minute rehearsal," said Mrs Hope. "Come on, you two."

Grandma Hope saw them to the door, and waved as they went off down the path. "Enjoy the party," she called. "I've made some cakes and biscuits for you, and I'll be dropping them off at the school tomorrow."

"Thanks, Gran," Mandy said, waving back.

"I wonder how Cobweb and Peaches are getting on?" said James as they walked the short distance to Willow Lane.

"Well, Tina said that Cobweb drank quite a lot of milk again this morning, while Peaches was licking her ears, of course!" Mandy said happily. "Isn't it brilliant, Mum? Peaches is really looking after Cobweb."

"It sounds like it's just what Cobweb needs," her mum agreed.

They arrived at the Cunninghams' house and James rang the bell. No one came for a few moments, and James was just about to ring it again when the door suddenly opened.

Matt stood in the doorway, looking worried. "Hi, come in," he said. "Sorry, we're in a bit of a mess at the moment. You won't believe this, but we've lost one of our mouse puppets!"

Mandy grinned at him. "No, you haven't," she said, taking the puppet out of the carrier bag Gran had wrapped it in. "Didn't Tina tell you? We took it away so my gran could mend it."

"Oh, yes, we heard all about *that*," said Matt. He took the puppet and looked at it closely. "Your gran's done a great job, Mandy. Please give her a big thank you from us."

"So what do you mean, you've lost a mouse puppet?" James asked curiously.

"I mean, we've lost the *other* one!" Matt groaned.

Mandy, James, and Mrs Hope stared at

him. "Oh no!" Mandy gasped.

Matt led Mandy, James and Mrs Hope inside. Tina, Mrs Cunningham and Alex were frantically searching the living-room. Tina and her mum were looking behind the sofa and armchairs while Alex was sorting through a big box of puppets. Dragons, witches and wizards lay on the carpet. Banjo and Freckle were scampering everywhere, weaving in and out of people's legs and having a great time.

"Shall we help you look?" offered James.

"Oh, please do," Alex sighed. "I don't know what we're going to do if we can't find this mouse. We don't have time to make another one."

"Where are Cobweb and Peaches?" Mandy asked Tina.

"In the box in the kitchen," replied Tina.

"I'll just go and say hello," Mandy said. "Then I'll help you search for the puppet."

She hurried off to the kitchen and peeped round the door, not wanting to disturb the kittens if they were asleep. But Cobweb and Peaches were both awake. They were sitting

bolt upright in the box, staring down at a small, white, furry thing with pink ears.

"Oh!" Mandy couldn't help smiling. "It's the missing mouse puppet!"

As Mandy watched, Peaches put out a paw and gently patted the mouse. Then she nudged it towards Cobweb. Cobweb immediately grabbed the mouse with her paw and began to sniff it.

Mandy burst out laughing. "I've found the mouse!" she called.

Everyone came dashing down the hall, and arrived in the kitchen just as Mandy rescued the puppet from the two kittens. Luckily, it hadn't been chewed or damaged at all.

"Peaches!" scolded Tina, trying to sound stern. "Did *you* take the mouse?"

Peaches began to purr loudly, not looking the least bit ashamed.

"Don't be too cross, Tina," Mandy said with a grin. "I think Peaches is just trying to get Cobweb to play. She's the best kitten nurse ever!"

# 10

## *New homes for Christmas*

"I'm full," declared James, pushing away his paper plate and patting his tummy. "I can't eat another thing!"

"Oh, aren't you going to have one of Gran's choc-chip buns?" Mandy said, pointing to a laden plate. "She made them especially for me to bring to the party."

"Well, maybe just one," said James,

pushing up his silver party hat which had fallen over one eye.

Mandy and Tina laughed. James had already eaten four sausage rolls, six sandwiches and three mince pies, not to mention several handfuls of crisps!

"Look, I think those are our stars hanging up over there," said Tina, nudging Mandy and pointing up at the ceiling.

Mandy nodded, and glanced around the school hall in delight. She thought it was the best Christmas party she'd ever been to. Every corner of the hall had been decorated by Mrs Cunningham and the other members of the PTA. A lofty Christmas tree stood in one corner, and at the far end of the hall was the puppet theatre, covered with a sparkly purple sheet so you couldn't tell what it was. Everyone in the hall was very excited, wondering what was going to happen, and Mandy, James and Tina had found it very hard not to let the secret out.

Once everyone had finished eating, Mrs Garvie, the headteacher, stood in front of the covered theatre and smiled warmly.

"And now for our surprise!" she announced. "I'd like you all to welcome *The Perfect Puppeteers*."

Everyone gasped and clapped loudly. Mandy, James and Tina grinned at each other as Matt and Alex appeared from behind the theatre in matching black outfits and pulled off the sheet with a dramatic flourish.

"Hello, Welford Primary School!" said Matt, with a low bow.

"Hello," the audience called excitedly.

Matt cupped a hand to his ear and frowned. "I didn't hear that, did you, Alex?" he said. "I thought we had an audience here somewhere!"

Alex shook her head. "I didn't hear anything either. Maybe they've all gone home!"

"Let's try again," Matt suggested, his eyes twinkling. "Hello, Welford Primary School!"

"HELLO!" This time everyone in the hall, including the teachers, joined in. The noise was deafening.

"Ah, that's better," said Alex with a grin.

"*The Perfect Puppeteers* would like to invite you to a performance of *Cinderella*. Prepare to be amazed and astounded!"

The audience clapped even harder, as Matt and Alex disappeared behind the puppet theatre again. Then, with a fanfare of trumpets blaring from a cassette machine, the show began. Cinderella popped up, wearing a dress of colourful rags. She started sweeping the kitchen and got told off by the two Ugly Sisters for not doing it properly. Her friend, Buttons, appeared beside her to sing a song to cheer her up.

The show was very funny, especially the Ugly Sister puppets. One wore a red wig which flew off every time she got angry, and the other had big round eyes which popped right out of her head.

Mandy, James and Tina were on the edge of their seats as they watched out for the scene when the Fairy Godmother had to get Cinderella ready for the ball. They couldn't wait to see the mice! When the Fairy Godmother waved her wand, and said, "Bring me two white mice," they held their breath and nudged each other.

Mandy stared hard at the two mice as they scampered on to the stage. It wasn't easy to tell which mouse was the one that Gran had mended, but then Mandy smiled to herself. One mouse's eyes were wider apart, making him look slightly surprised. Mandy guessed that *that* was the one Gran had mended. She must have sewn the eye back on a tiny bit further over than it should be.

James seemed to have spotted exactly the same thing. "I think that surprised-looking

mouse is the one your gran mended," he whispered.

"Wouldn't *you* look surprised if you were going to be turned into a horse?" Mandy laughed as, with a puff of glittering smoke, the two mice disappeared and a pair of beautiful white horses took their place.

Mandy, James and Tina were also keen to see the scene where the smoke bomb was let off and the pumpkin changed into a coach. Even though they knew how it was done, they gasped along with the rest of the audience as smoke filled the stage and the pumpkin vanished, to be quickly replaced by the gleaming golden coach.

"They're brilliant, aren't they?" James whispered to Mandy, as the audience clapped loudly. Mandy nodded, too busy watching the show to reply.

There was more applause as Cinderella changed from her rags into a beautiful silver dress and went off to the ball. Buttons was left behind in the kitchen and he sang another song, this time with the audience's help. Alex came out to pin the words to the front of the puppet theatre. The song was full of tongue-twisters, and soon everyone was laughing so much they could hardly get the words out. At the end of the song, Buttons started throwing sweets into the audience, and everyone scrambled to get one.

"Look out, Tina!" Mandy grinned, catching a toffee as it flew towards them.

The final scene was the wedding of Cinderella and the Prince, and there were loud cheers as Cinderella appeared in her white wedding dress to take a bow.

"That was great!" said James, clapping as hard as he could.

"I think everyone liked it, didn't they?" said Tina, looking round the hall at all the smiling faces.

"Of course they did!" Mandy replied.

Matt and Alex appeared from behind the theatre for one last time, and bowed to the audience.

"Thank you very much," said Matt. "We're really glad you enjoyed the show."

"Now *we* want to say a special thank you,"

Alex added. "If it wasn't for some good friends of ours, we wouldn't have had any white mice in the show today. And then how would Cinderella have got to the ball? So Mandy, James and Tina, thank you!"

"It was great, Gran," Mandy said, as she, James and Grandma Hope walked through Welford. Gran had come to pick them up after the party and to collect her cake tins. "The mouse looked lovely, didn't he, James?"

James nodded. "And it was really funny, Mrs Hope," he told her. "One of the Ugly Sisters wore a wig which kept whizzing off, and once it landed on Mrs Garvie's lap!"

"The food was brilliant," Mandy added. "And then we had party games after the puppet show."

Gran laughed. "You won't be wanting any tea then," she said as they turned into Willow Lane.

"Well, maybe just a snack," Mandy said, grinning at James who was looking disappointed.

As they walked past the Cunninghams' house towards Lilac Cottage, the door flew open and Tina rushed out. She was red in the face and looked very excited. "Mandy! James!" she called. "I'm glad I saw you. I've got something really brilliant to tell you!"

"What is it?" asked James.

"Come inside and I'll tell you," Tina said, beaming.

"You got home quickly," Mandy remarked, as they walked up to the front door.

"Uncle Matt and Alex brought me home in their van with all the puppet stuff," Tina explained. "Come in."

Feeling very curious, Mandy and James went into the living-room, followed by Mandy's gran. The room was as cosy and welcoming as ever, with the Christmas tree twinkling in the corner. Mrs Cunningham was sitting on the sofa, and Matt and Alex were on their knees in front of the fire, playing with Banjo and Freckle. They were dangling a bit of silver tinsel over the kittens' heads, and Banjo and Freckle were trying to grab it. Peaches and Cobweb were curled up in front of the fire, purring, and as usual Peaches was giving the grey kitten a good wash.

"Mum and Dad have said that I can keep Cobweb!" Tina burst out, her eyes shining. "They said that she and Peaches get on so well, it would be a shame to split them up."

"That's great!" Mandy gasped. She'd been worrying about finding the right home for fragile little Cobweb, but now the problem was solved.

"And guess what?" Alex chimed in. "Matt and I have fallen in love with these two." She pointed at Freckle and Banjo. "And we're going to keep them! We've spoken to the Devlins, and they're really happy about it."

Mandy beamed and turned to James. "It looks like we can take those posters down now. The kittens have all got new homes!"

At that moment the doorbell rang and Mrs Cunningham went to see who it was. She came back with the Devlins, who were carrying three wicker cat baskets and three bright red tartan blankets.

"Hello, everyone," smiled Mr Devlin. "We thought we'd bring round a little Christmas present for the kittens – and their new owners! Look, new baskets and blankets for all of them."

"Let's see if they like them," said Mrs Devlin, putting the baskets down and tucking the blankets inside. Everyone watched as Banjo and Freckle jumped into two of the baskets and began to explore every corner, sniffing eagerly with their tails held straight up like tiny flags. Cobweb was a bit more wary, but after Peaches had given her a gentle nudge with her nose, she climbed into the third basket and settled down with her paws tucked underneath her.

"I think they like them!" said Tina.

Peaches looked rather put out that *she* didn't have a basket too. She padded over to Cobweb's basket, sniffed at it, then squeezed in next to the grey kitten. It was a bit of a tight fit, but neither kitten seemed to mind. They snuggled down together, curling their

bodies around each other. Peaches began to purr loudly, and licked Cobweb's ears.

"Merry Christmas, Peaches," Mandy laughed, kneeling down by the basket to stroke her. "And it looks like your kitten kisses have made it a really merry Christmas for Cobweb, too!"

# LUCY DANIELS

### Animal Ark Pets

| | | | |
|---|---|---|---|
| 0 340 67283 8 | Puppy Puzzle | £3.99 | ❏ |
| 0 340 67284 6 | Kitten Crowd | £3.99 | ❏ |
| 0 340 67285 4 | Rabbit Race | £3.99 | ❏ |
| 0 340 67286 2 | Hamster Hotel | £3.99 | ❏ |
| 0 340 68729 0 | Mouse Magic | £3.99 | ❏ |
| 0 340 68730 4 | Chick Challenge | £3.99 | ❏ |
| 0 340 68731 2 | Pony Parade | £3.99 | ❏ |
| 0 340 68732 0 | Guinea-pig Gang | £3.99 | ❏ |
| 0 340 71371 2 | Gerbil Genius | £3.99 | ❏ |
| 0 340 71372 0 | Duckling Diary | £3.99 | ❏ |
| 0 340 71373 9 | Lamb Lessons | £3.99 | ❏ |
| 0 340 71374 7 | Doggy Dare | £3.99 | ❏ |
| 0 340 73585 6 | Donkey Derby | £3.99 | ❏ |
| 0 340 73586 4 | Hedgehog Home | £3.99 | ❏ |
| 0 340 73587 2 | Frog Friends | £3.99 | ❏ |
| 0 340 73588 0 | Bunny Bonanza | £3.99 | ❏ |
| 0 340 73589 9 | Ferret Fun | £3.99 | ❏ |
| 0 340 73590 2 | Rat Riddle | £3.99 | ❏ |
| 0 340 73592 9 | Cat Crazy | £3.99 | ❏ |
| 0 340 73605 4 | Pets' Party | £3.99 | ❏ |
| 0 340 73593 7 | Foal Frolics | £3.99 | ❏ |
| 0 340 77861 X | Piglet Pranks | £3.99 | ❏ |
| 0 340 77878 4 | Spaniel Surprise | £3.99 | ❏ |
| 0 340 85204 6 | Horse Hero | £3.99 | ❏ |
| 0 340 85205 4 | Calf Capers | £3.99 | ❏ |
| 0 340 85206 2 | Puppy Prizes | £3.99 | ❏ |

*All Hodder Children's books are available at your local bookshop, or can be ordered direct from the publisher. Just tick the titles you would like and complete the details below. Prices and availability are subject to change without prior notice.*

Please enclose a cheque or postal order made payable to *Bookpoint Ltd*, and send to: Hodder Children's Books, 39 Milton Park, Abingdon, OXON OX14 4TD, UK. Email Address: orders@bookpoint.co.uk

If you would prefer to pay by credit card, our call centre team would be delighted to take your order by telephone. Our direct line *01235 400414* (lines open 9.00 am–6.00 pm Monday to Saturday, 24 hour message answering service). Alternatively you can send a fax on *01235 400454*.

| TITLE | | FIRST NAME | | SURNAME | |
|---|---|---|---|---|---|

| ADDRESS | |
|---|---|
| | |
| | |
| | |

| DAYTIME TEL: | | POST CODE | |
|---|---|---|---|

If you would prefer to pay by credit card, please complete:
Please debit my Visa/Access/Diner's Card/American Express (delete as applicable) card no:

| | | | | | | | | | | | | | | | |
|---|---|---|---|---|---|---|---|---|---|---|---|---|---|---|---|

Signature ..................................................... Expiry Date: ..................................

If you would NOT like to receive further information on our products please tick the box. ❏